Festive Fun
Christmas
Activity Book

This book belongs to

_____

Wonder House

T0206803

Dear Santa,

My name is _____

I am _____ years old

and live in _____

For Christmas, I would like

_____

Thank you, Santa!

Be Creative

Make this chilling Christmas Eve look stunning by drawing trees on the tree stumps and decorate them.

Christmas Carols

The choir is merrily singing Christmas Carols. Trace the words to find out what they are singing.

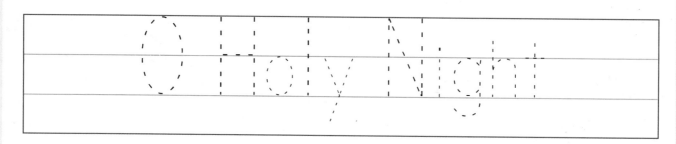

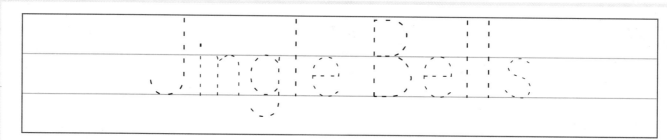

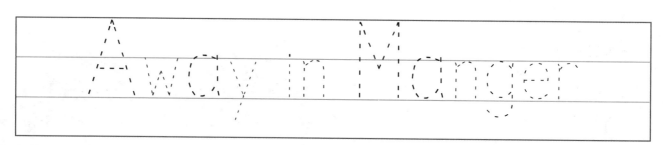

Christmas Wish List

I wonder, what's there on Bob, Alex and Laura's Christmas wish list? Follow the lines to find out what each of them want for Christmas.

Splendid Stockings

Make a wish and color the giant stocking with colors of your choice.

May all your wishes come true!

Count the stockings in each row and write their number in the circles.

Christmas Shopping

It's Christmas Shopping time! Find and circle seven differences between the two Christmas market scenes.

Find the Sleigh

Cute little reindeer has lost its way. Let's help it find its path to the sleigh. Use the code key to guide you.

Oh Deer!

Draw antlers of the deer using your hands.

Lights Up

Color the lights as per the pattern.

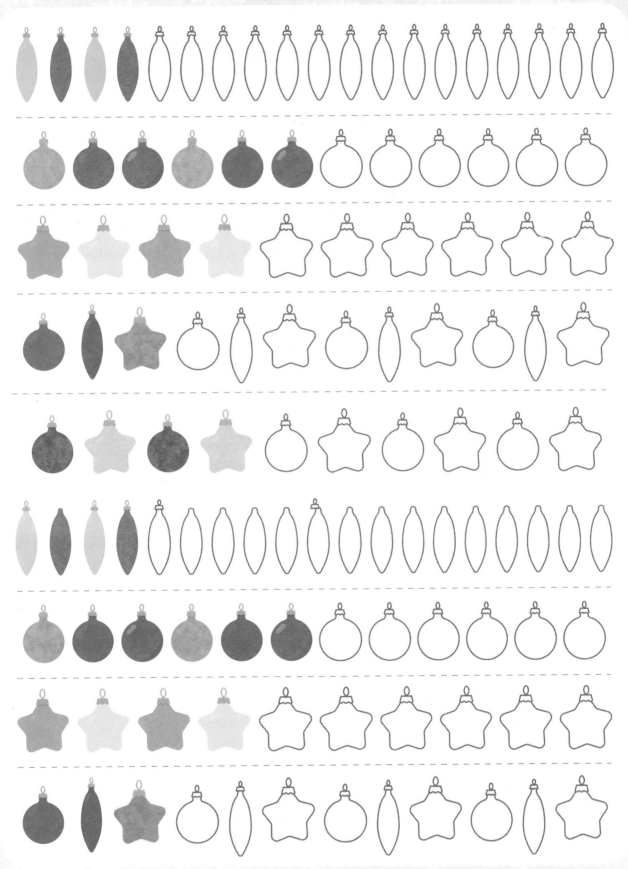

Busy Christmas Street

Find out how many each of the given things are. Write your answers in the boxes.

Animals ☐

Presents ☐

Cars ☐

Wheels ☐

Trees ☐

13

I Spy

I spy with my little eye. Can you also spy with your eye? Santa is playing 'I Spy' with the animals. Find and circle all the animals you see here.

Budding Artist

Carefully observe and draw the picture of Santa in the grid.

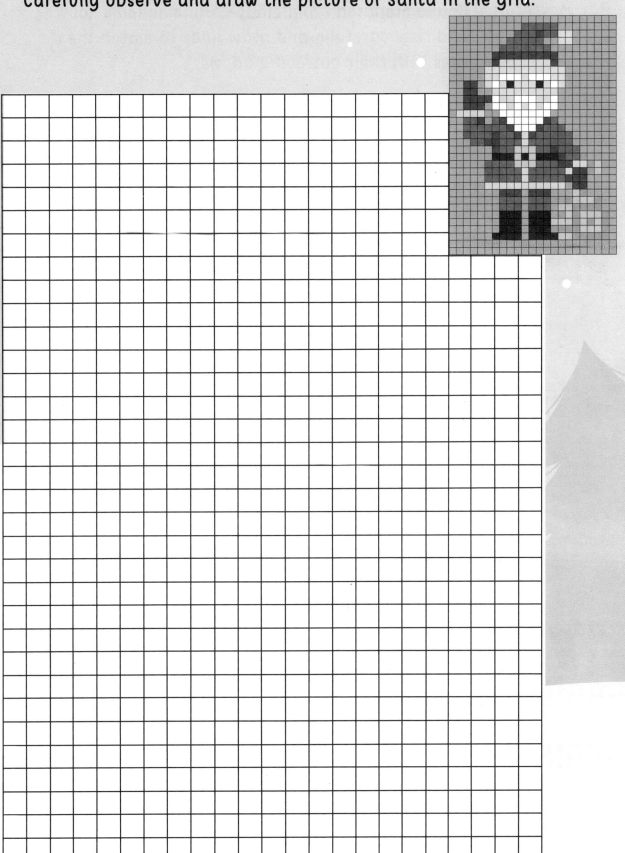

Our Master Chefs have prepared a delicious Christmas feast for Santa. Observe the dishes carefully and draw lines to match the dishes with their correct shadows.

Christmas Fun

Join the dots and take out your colors. Decorate the page using the color code.

Color Code:

1	**4**
2	**5**
3	

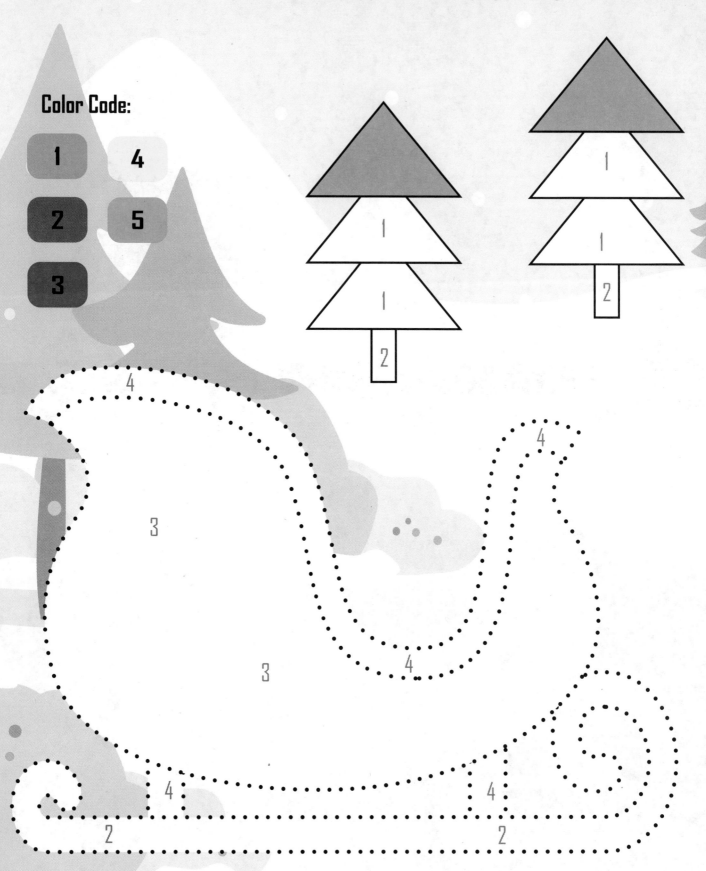

Lead the Way

Help the Three Wise Men reach Baby Jesus through the desert maze.

FINISH

Penguin Quest

Observe the Penguins and find the following.

A) a penguin wearing glasses
B) a penguin with a cake
C) a dancing penguin
D) a penguin eating candy

Ho! Ho! Ho!

Santa Claus has come bearing presents. But something is amiss. Paste cotton balls on his beard to make it look fluffy.

Merry Mix-up

Christmas items have got mixed together. Count each of them and write their number in the boxes.

Baking News

Splash colors in the given picture to make the bakery look appealing.

Fancy Wardrobe

Peppy has a really nice collection of clothes in his wardrobe for Christmas. Let's find out what clothes he has.
Find the given clothes in the grid.

Cap
Gloves

Sweater
Scarf

Boots
Jacket

a	C	B	o	a	a	a	G
c	a	k	o	t	e	o	l
J	p	S	w	s	s	v	e
a	y	y	e	a	y	l	s
c	k	e	w	t	w	p	e
k	a	t	h	e	r	r	s
S	c	e	i	r	t	e	j
o	a	r	f	n	s	o	o

Hint: Follow the capital letters.

Christmas Crossword

Using the picture clues complete the crossword.

1.

2.

3.

4.

5.

6.

1 S
 L

2 E
3 E 4
5 K
W
6 S A

ANSWER: 1.Snowglobe 2.Deer 3.Present 4.Snowman 5.Stocking 6.Santa

28

Perfect Presents

Santa has fulfilled the wishes of Joy, Adam, Tim and Joseph. Find out what they have got by tracing the lines.

Let's Cheer Up Santa!

Splash the picture with vibrant colors to make Santa happy!

Gingerbread Town

Help the three friends go through the maze to the gingerbread house.

Wish you a Beary Christmas

Can you find out which two Polar Bears are similar? Draw a line to match them.

Follow the steps and learn to draw the Christmas tree. Draw and color as many Christmas trees as you want.

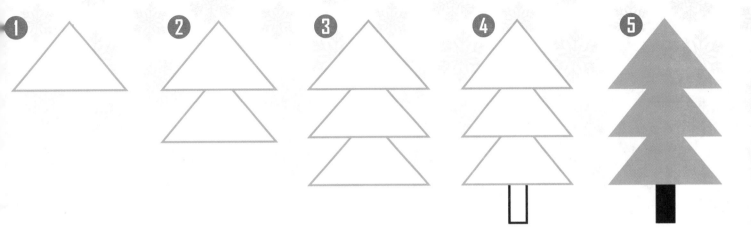

Snack Attack

The hungry animals can't wait to eat the delicious Christmas snacks. Hurry! Trace the lines with different color pencils to find out who will eat what before they attack the snacks.

Green and Bright

Join the dots and color the tree and the decorations using the color code.

Color Code:

1
2
3
4

Stocking Search

Draw lines to connect the stockings that have similar colors and patterns.

Christmas Wordsearch

Look at these pictures, read their names aloud and find them in the grid below.

 present   bell   candle   chocolate

 star   toys   tree

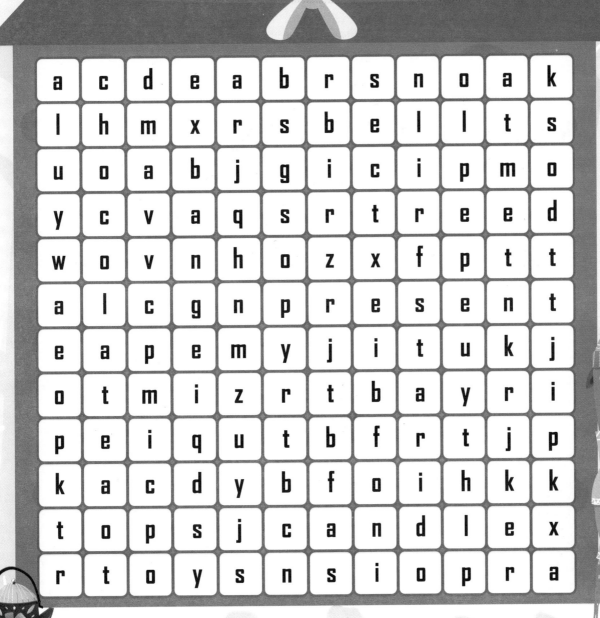

a	c	d	e	a	b	r	s	n	o	a	k
l	h	m	x	r	s	b	e	l	l	t	s
u	o	a	b	j	g	i	c	i	p	m	o
y	c	v	a	q	s	r	t	r	e	e	d
w	o	v	n	h	o	z	x	f	p	t	t
a	l	c	g	n	p	r	e	s	e	n	t
e	a	p	e	m	y	j	i	t	u	k	j
o	t	m	i	z	r	t	b	a	y	r	i
p	e	i	q	u	t	b	f	r	t	j	p
k	a	c	d	y	b	f	o	i	h	k	k
t	o	p	s	j	c	a	n	d	l	e	x
r	t	o	y	s	n	s	i	o	p	r	a

Snowman Fun

Join the dots and complete the snowman.

Ready, Set, Glow!

Let's decorate the Christmas tree. Check if all the things mentioned below are there and circle them.

4

Stars

1

Gingerbreadman

2

Candy Canes

3

Stockings

Christmas Chaos

Mr Brown's Christmas Gift Store is messy. Let's help him out in arranging the things properly. Circle the things that don't belong on each shelf.

Christmas Collection

Count and write the number of each Christmas goody.

How Many Deer?

There are a lot of lovely reindeer in Santa's kingdom.
Count and write the total numbers of reindeer in:

| Blue | .... | Red | .... |

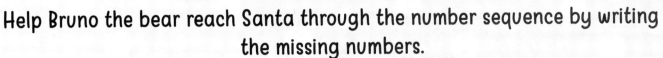

Search for Santa

Help Bruno the bear reach Santa through the number sequence by writing the missing numbers.

Christmas Pattern

Complete the Christmas pattern.

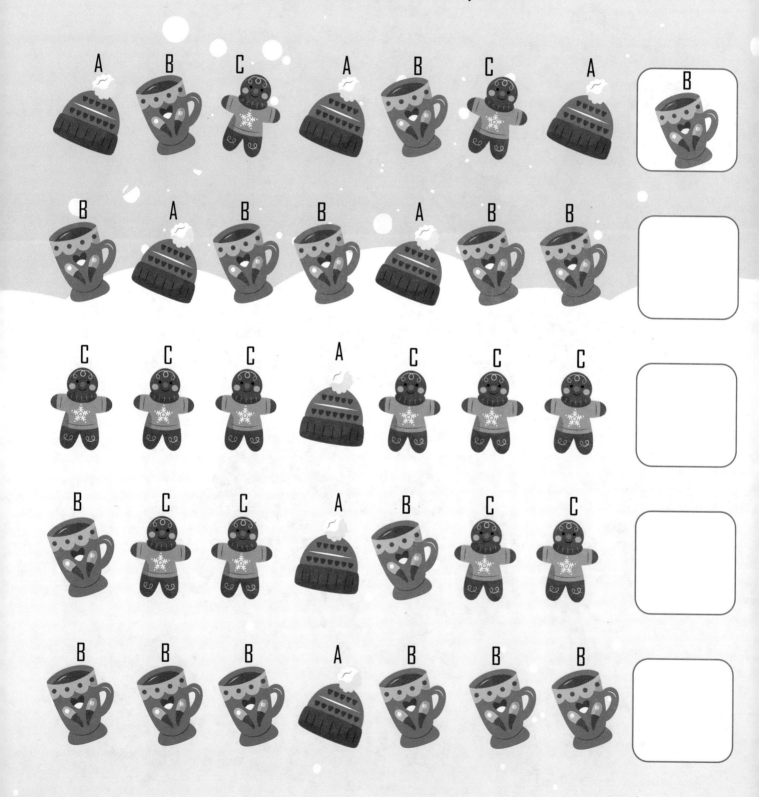

Christmas Sudoku

Fill in the empty boxes to complete the Christmas sudoku.

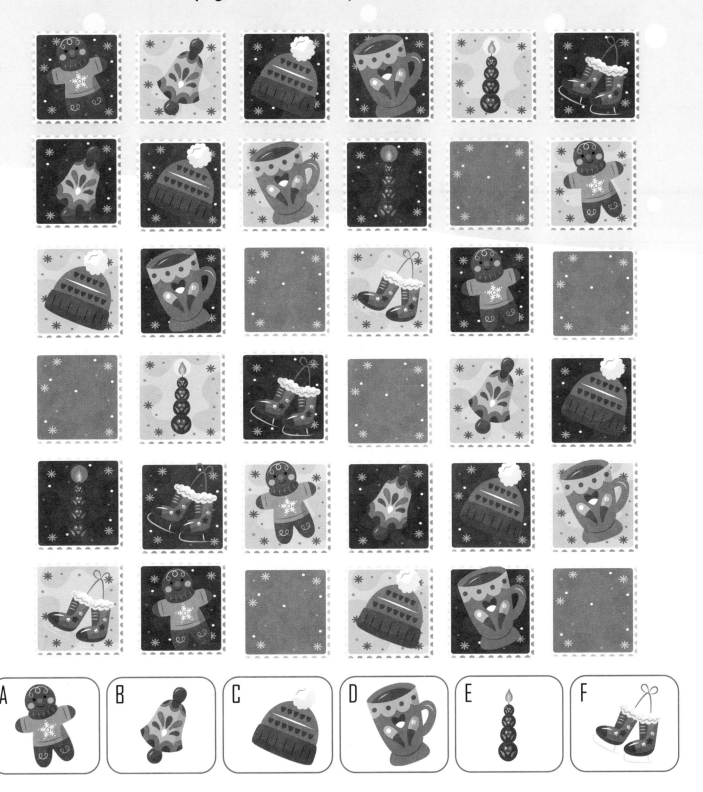

Learn to draw gingerbread cookies. In the given space try making your own.

How to Draw

Observe and make your own snow flakes in the given space.

Learn how to draw a snowman. Let's make your own in the given space.

How to Draw

Observe and draw your snow globe in the given space.

Finger Prints

Look at the pictures below. Make similar pictures using your thumbprint on the opposite page to complete them.

Christmas Doodle

Color the doodles inside the jar.

Christmas Bells

Color the jingling Christmas bells with bright colors.

Connect the Dots

Join the dots and color the image.

Santa's Bag

Paste stickers to see what is in Santa's bag.

Can you Find

Observe the image and find everything given at the bottom of the page.

Gingerbread House

Use earbuds to color the circles and semi-circles given in the picture.

Christmas Style

Using stickers dress your gingerbread men.

Family Outing

Paste the photographs of your family members.

Christmas holidays are here!

Monday

Tuesday

Wednesday

Thursday

How will your plan your week?

Friday

Saturday

Sunday

Gift Ideas

What will you gift your loved ones this Christmas?

Mom

Dad

Sis

Bro

Grandma

Grandpa

Best Friend

Memo

What will you have in your holiday menu?

Meals for the Week

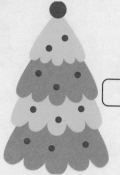

Christmas Bucket List

☐ Decorate the Christmas tree

☐ Buy the perfect tree

☐ Light up the house

☐ Hang a flower wreath on the door

☐ Buy candy canes

☐ Choose scented candles

☐ Wear Christmas socks

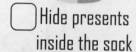

☐ Hide presents inside the sock

☐ Sing 'jingle bells' with friends

☐ Wear santa hat

☐ Make handmade crafts

☐ Visit santa!

☐ Make a bucket list for santa

☐ Make a snow angel

☐ Make gingerbread cookies

☐ A hot tea for Christmas Eve

☐ Buy presents

☐ Make Christmas cards

☐ Send out Christmas cards

Christmas Wish List

I've waited patiently all year for...

My favorite things are...

_____

_____

_____

_____

_____

_____

I want to visit...

My wish for someone else this Christmas...

Christmas Greetings

Write a Christmas message for your friend. Use the given stamps to decorate your letter.

From

_____
_____
_____
_____

Merry Christmas

To

_____
_____
_____
_____

Better in Sweaters

Observe the color codes and color the sweaters.

Meals with Family

Paste the correct stickers of the food shown above and complete the picture.

Mood Tracker

How are you feeling? Choose the color balls as per your mood to decorate the tree.

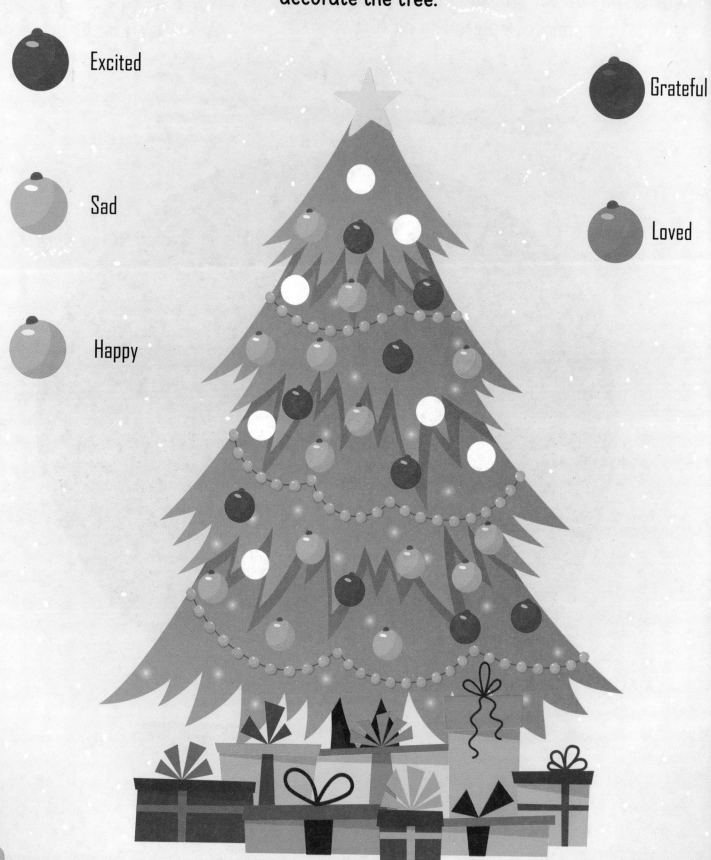

Excited

Sad

Happy

Grateful

Loved

Cut out Masks

Cut out the given masks and make your Christmas party much more fun.

Paper Christmas Tree

Use fingerprint coloring to decorate your Christmas tree.
Cut out the tree following the dots and stick the edges with glue.

Colors Code

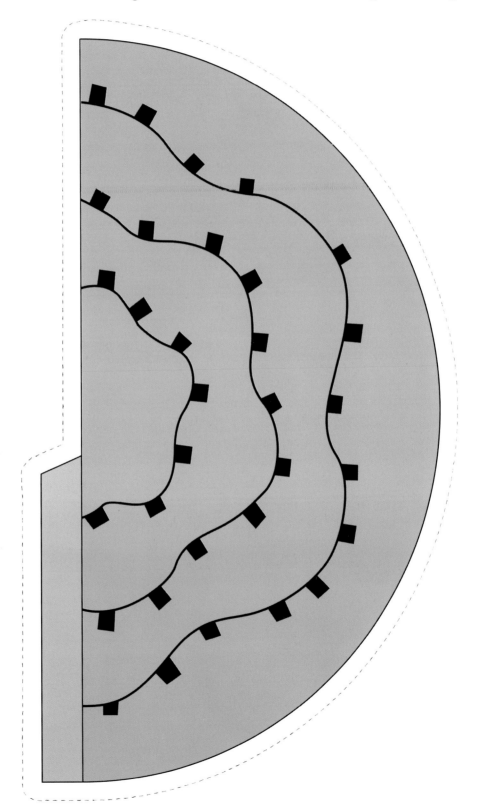

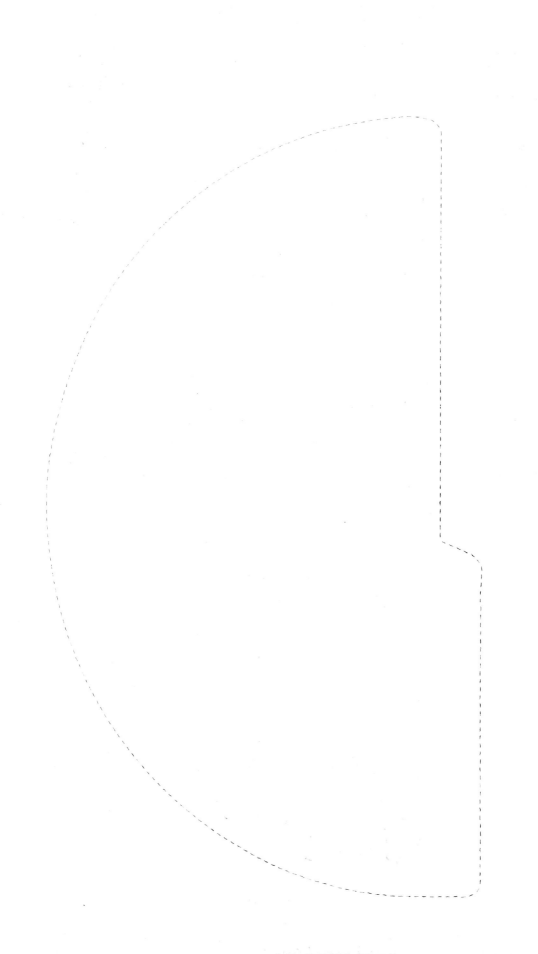

Finger Puppets

Cut out the given animals, wrap them around your fingers using glue and weave amazing stories.

Pretend and Play

Cut out the given images. Paste A with A, back to back. Do the same for the other alphabets. Cut along the dotted lines.
Now, carefully see the complete images, assemble your cut out in similar manner.

D

C

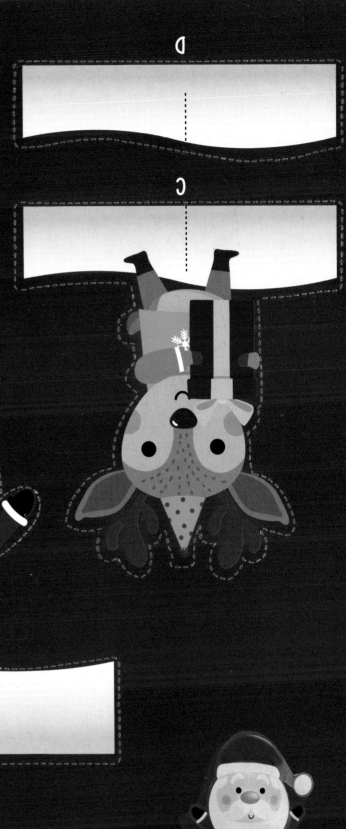

A

B

E

F

G

H

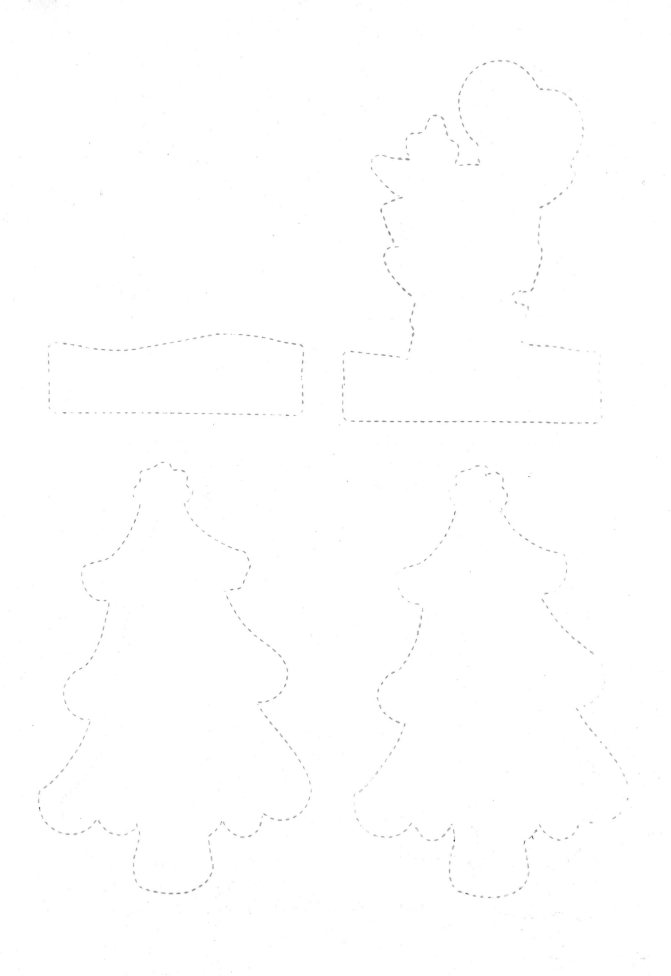

E

F

G

H

Page 57

Page 68

Page 71

MERRY CHRISTMAS

HAPPY HOLIDAYS

merry
CHRISTMAS
Happy New Year

merry
CHRISTMAS
Happy New Year

merry
CHRISTMAS
Happy New Year

Merry CHRISTMAS

HAPPY NEW YEAR

merry
CHRISTMAS
Happy New Year

MERRY CHRISTMAS

HAPPY HOLIDAYS

merry
CHRISTMAS
Happy New Year

Merry CHRISTMAS

HAPPY NEW YEAR

merry
CHRISTMAS
Happy New Year

merry
CHRISTMAS
Happy New Year

Merry CHRISTMAS

HAPPY NEW YEAR

Festive Fun
Christmas
Activity Book

Christmas is the time to be with family and be joyful. This activity book celebrates the Christmas spirit. So, be joyful and merry as you enjoy the activities in the book. From coloring to mazes to learning to draw to pasting stickers and even making masks, this activity book is all-inclusive and loaded with fun.

Copyright © 2023 Wonder House Books
Wonder House Books is an imprint of Prakash Books

ISBN: 978-93-54406-19-5   CAN 13.99

9 789354 406195

www.wonderhousebooks.com   000999039900